My Secret Place

For my patient family, but
most especially for my
nephew David

Inquiries should be addressed to Lothrop, Lee & Shepard Books, a division of William Morrow & Company, Inc., 1350 Avenue of the Americas, New York, New York 10019. Printed in Hong Kong.

First Edition 1 2 3 4 5 6 7 8 9 10

Library of Congress Cataloging in Publication Data
Magnus, Erica. My secret place / by Erica Magnus.
p. cm. Summary: Describes a secret place for just one person and Bear.
ISBN 0-688-11859-3.—ISBN 0-688-11860-7 (lib. bdg.) [1. Solitude—Fiction.
2. Bears—Fiction.] I. Title. PZ7.M2737My 1994 [E]—dc20 93-8701 CIP AC

My Secret Place

by Erica Magnus

Lothrop, Lee & Shepard Books New York

My secret place is just for me — and Bear.
There we eat my pinecone stew

and when we're through,
we round up cows

or slay a dragon.

We search for magic stones

that grow us into giants

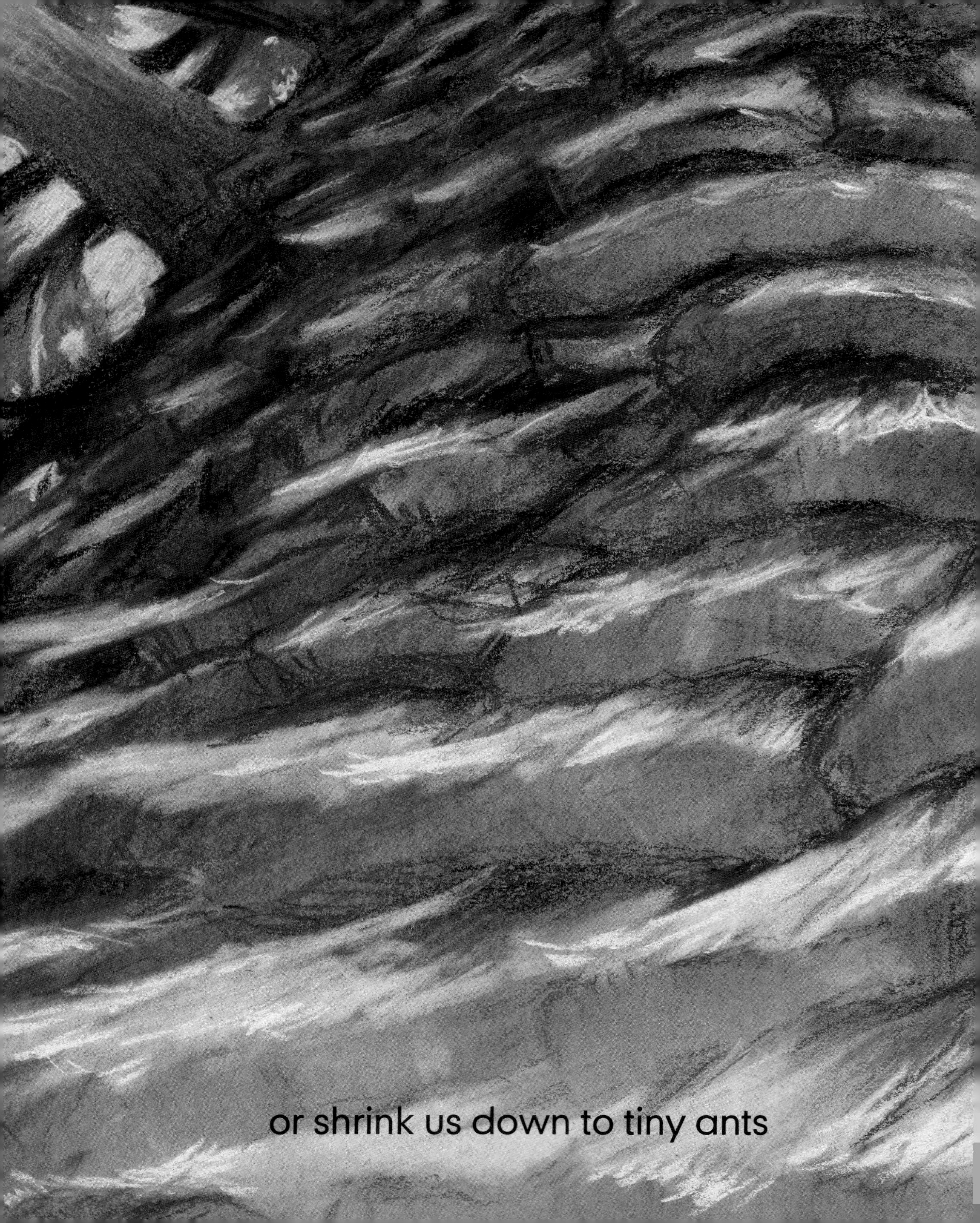

or shrink us down to tiny ants

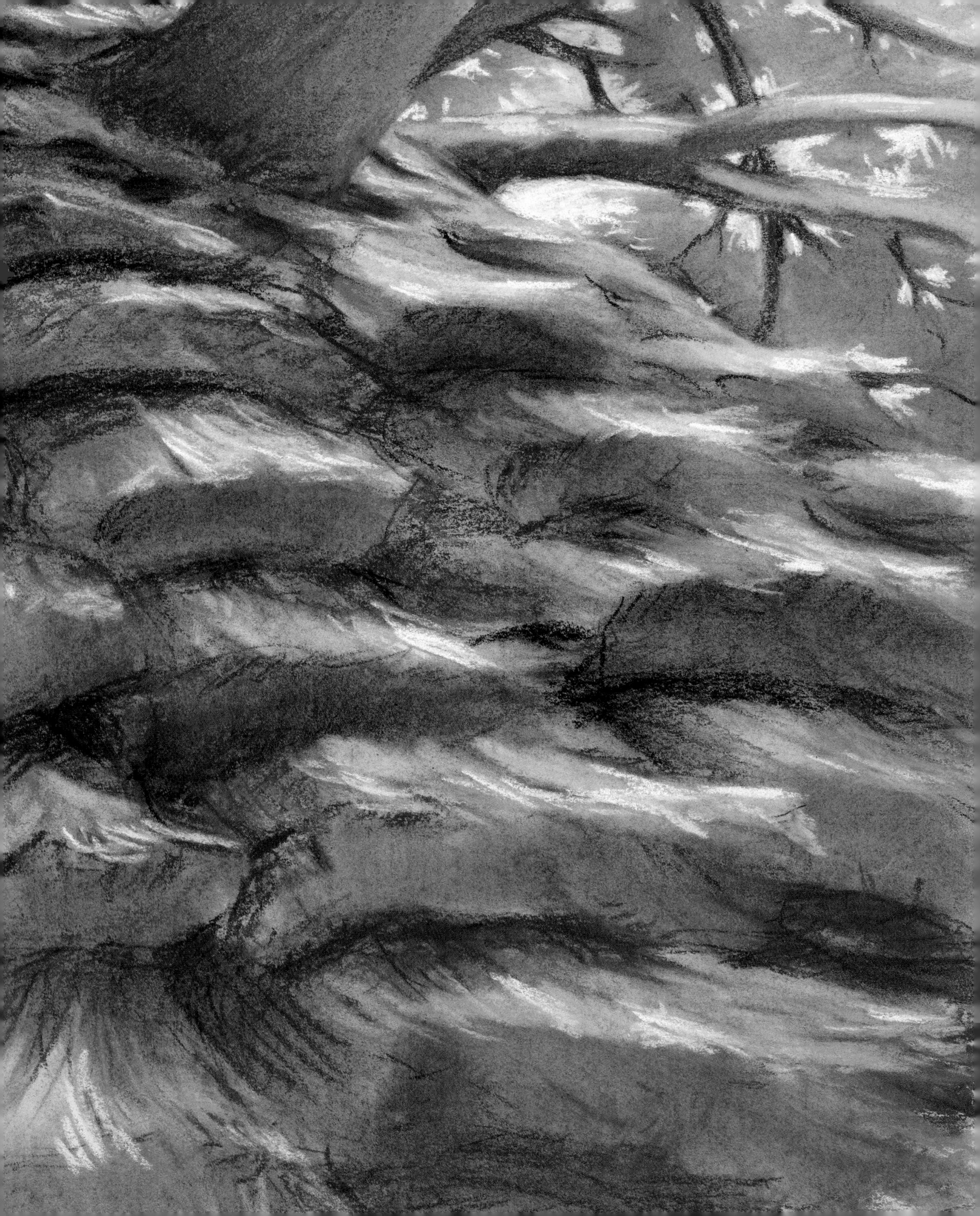

or let us fly like birds!

And if the wind turns all the leaves silver side up,
and dark clouds gather in the sky,

the rain won't find us bears

in our cozy den,

in my secret place.